6/15

Mitchell Goes Driving

Hallie Durand

illustrated by Tony Fucile

CANDLEWICK PRESS

Mitchell never ever EVER wanted to go to bed.
Until his dad finally said he could drive there.

Mitchell was three years, nine months, and
five days old when he got his license.

REMOTE-CONTROL DAD
DRIVER'S LICENSE

12876 77780 857873

MITCHELL
BOX 9085
SILVER MOUNTAIN ROAD

SEX   HGT   EYES
M   3-02   BRN

Mitchell

First, he inspected his new car's tires.

"Good," said Mitchell.

Then he checked the engine.

"Good," said Mitchell.

And he hopped into the driver's seat.

The windshield looked a little dirty.

So Mitchell wiped it off.

"Shiny!" said Mitchell.

His car was an automatic, so Mitchell put it right into drive.

His car could go fast!

VROOM!

Ruh-roh.

Mitchell put his car into reverse,

shifted into neutral, and coasted to bed.

The next night, Mitchell remembered to stop and look both ways.

He also learned how to beep the horn.
He liked the way it sounded . . . a lot!

Mitchell could make a left

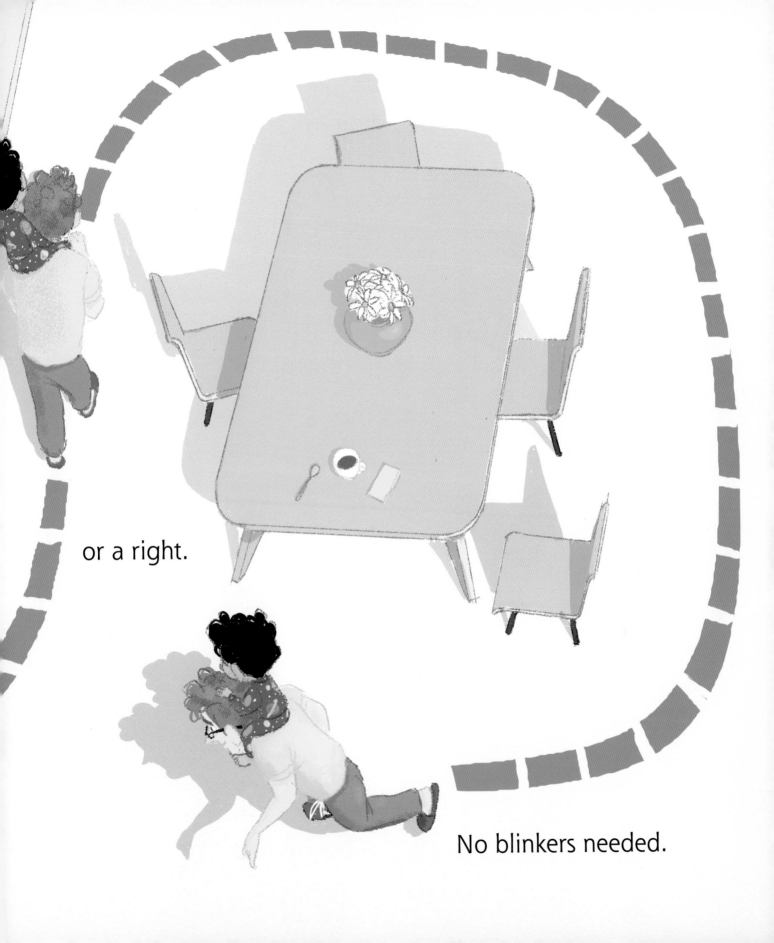

or a right.

No blinkers needed.

And now Mitchell knew just when to press the brakes so there weren't any more collisions.

Mitchell felt comfortable behind the wheel.
In fact, he loved driving to bed!

The next night, even before his bedtime,
Mitchell went to get his car.

"You need some oil," he said.

And he poured in some oil.

The car was sputtering a little, but Mitchell didn't mind.

"You're OK," he said as he closed the hood.

Then he hopped into the driver's seat and backed the car out of the garage.

He slowed down for the speed bumps in the driveway,

but when he merged onto the open road, he really got going.

Mitchell was a great driver now, handling the hairpin turns and staying in his lane, even in two-way traffic.

They had driven a long way when Mitchell noticed that the gas tank was on Empty.

"You need gas," said Mitchell.

Mitchell and his car took three right turns, then a left, and beeped the horn six times.

BEEP! BEEP!
BEEP! BEEP!
BEEP!
BEEP!

Mitchell turned on his headlights and
pulled up to the cookie jar.

"This is the gas station," he said.

"No," said the car.

Mitchell was surprised. The car had never spoken before.

"We need gas," said Mitchell. "Gas is a cookie."

"No gas," said the car.
"YES GAS!" said Mitchell, and he turned on his hazards.
This was an emergency.

And that's when Mitchell's car did a U-turn

and took a shortcut, straight to Mitchell's bed.

"Will we drive again tomorrow?" said Mitchell.
"As long as you stay on the road," said Dad.

And then Mitchell's dad tucked his driver in . . .

and Mitchell drove off to find that
gas station in his dreams.

For Michael Alan Steiner, the original Remote-Control Dad
H. D.

For Eli and Elinor
T. F.

First paperback edition 2013

Published in hardcover as *Mitchell's License*

Library of Congress Cataloging-in-Publication Data is available.
Library of Congress Catalog Card Number 2010039181
ISBN 978-0-7636-4496-3 (hardcover)
ISBN 978-0-7636-6737-5 (paperback)

13 14 15 16 17 18 SCP 10 9 8 7 6 5 4 3 2 1

Printed in Humen, Dongguan, China

This book was typeset in Shannon.
The illustrations were done digitally.

Candlewick Press
99 Dover Street
Somerville, Massachusetts 02144

visit us at www.candlewick.com